The poems in the collection you are holding have been drawn from four sources:

The Fool Chains (1997)

Fake Like A Moon (2016)

The Tree Knew (2018)

On Opening The Spring Dream (2020)

The author has also published three novels and one play.

Each Code Remains (2018)

The Great Storm (2019)

Obviation (2019)

Je Suis Votre Mauvaise Conscience (2020)

For Béatrice

Chapter 1:   On Opening The Spring Dream

On opening the spring dream
of the cliff, the nest and the ledge
lapped between the curling cedar bone
my future grief scribbled as a worm.
The knotted cloth nailed on our root
that made the blond head green
and seasoned from the hidden suns
I flicked reeds into the dunes
my unstamped envelope unstuck.

On opening the spring dream
before a flare of iode gills, and steps
sunken as the trench beneath an eye
the shredding scales we grew and handed down
with the black, hard tendrils still inside the pouch.
My north wind seldom drowns
the keening stumps whole,
but trips on broken ropes
its next prints washed out before

On opening the spring dream

for her smile, the edge of a lip – flaking saffron
bent in to sing the indolence of crush
and arm-hairs pricked and freckled ghosts
reflecting down from each lost drip.
The broken boy whose combing brings the twig,
buds sand-taught rivers in the heart.

On opening the spring dream whole
we must not wake it.

Chapter 2:   Currents

The kick back from the current hides a treasure no
man knows

Lying beneath the stones

Every son in drowning waves

Currents stay, currents stay

The tales we heard as infants tend to satisfy our crime

Felt in lashes in the day

As each memory attests

Currents fade, currents fade

A song that came from deeper the intent to pull you
in

As a howling from a cave

Sometime hanging, never saved

Currents sway, currents sway

The lips that hid the yellow teeth and leering of the
maid

Poisoned many a friend

You would well understand

As you played, As you played

An ocean filled with darkness mere reflections of
within

Foaming over our graves

And you now read all names

Currents stay, currents stay

Chapter 3:   Storms Cradle to Me

Storms cradled to me

Everyone sees

Nobody dared

Grinding your metal to leaves

Freeing a curse words are your lairs

Laughs canned in a shot

Fake like a moon

Escaping the dusk

Turning attention inside

Racks upon bones begin to rust

Lives grown through a rock

Roots all in knots

Nooses so tight

Reach down your soul is at peace

Lost in the mortal grip of the night

Then here we awake

All was mere fright

We are not dead

Standing we release the fear

If this was not real, why did nobody say

Chapter 4:   The Last Box Of Magic

The rain paid my bills on condition
I'd never return here
and the ghosts of the honeymoon choir
are still gathering light
pushing branches of gorse to the east as we enter the
season
there are several miles until winter can summon its
night

In the back seat the papers are crushed
and displayed now as puzzles
from the centre the dust has formed statues
to worship the cost
and the clicking of lights
that would always feel safe as you slumber
now the haunting of thunder,
the last box of magic you lost

While three rows have been cleared
for processions of unfallen harvest
and the distance respected the ages
and who could recall

there's a space between words
and the consequent field of their laughter
and the joke is on you
since the moment your idea was born

When the tears have decided
there's no more destruction to gather
when the heartbreak has turned you to sand
that the rains now erode
when the tunnel leads back
to the old weathered harbour in silence
when the sea gulls face southwards
you'll understand you have made home

Chapter 5:   Hildeburgh's Isles

In always its wind
Erosion will bring
Your isle split in three
Your memory free

You'll sink into sands
Clouds all facing down
Through up-facing hands
It is winter all round

The middle eye and
The mainland empty
Nowhere there and
No way home
The endless sky
Horizons plenty
No one sees you and
No one knows

In seasons just one
All flattened in mud
Your shale cast away
For features you wait

Life-time basking in
A moon for no nights
A sea with no tides
A life with no size

Chapter 6:   Empty Earth

Tired branch

willowed down

to the shrieking soil

births

head on now

freshly buried cold

figurines knee to hand

feet paddle the sands

howl out

treason now,

set the curtains high

Grim rains

stringing waves of dusk

up into our sky

fates hide inside towers

shadows bark mountains ours'

And empty earth shoots out weeds

never again never to leave

here's what you need

here are your rooms

here you are me

I tried

saving souls

but no rains arrived

down hill

empty earth

feeding all our lies

statues up in a day

though the stars cheer again

Chapter 7:   Faces in spume

Features washed into the sands
Dried up in lines I reach for your hand
And shells crumble back to glass
Their fossilized creature lives are past
Their voices fill the room
With faces in the spume

The mud creeps round my toes
Sand in between each tooth grows
In streams that lead me back to sea
Vulnerable lives away from me
The choice is only gloom
And faces in the spume

Webbed prints upon the beach
Water's priests that nature keeps
And urchins, crabs and all that move
The forests lost no pasts to prove
Their roots are all they do
Their faces in the spume

Chapter 8:   no words

the curtains are closed
there are no words
the lights are on
night has fallen
there are no words
buckles, blinds, covers
there is silence
black paper, violence
there is nothing
just a dog barking in a lane
a dripping down the window pane
the fake smile queen
in the corner
the curtains are closed
there are no words

Chapter 9:   The Winding Of Worlds

Travel with me

Take my lead

The winding of worlds goes unseen

Everybody has their day

The danger will hide in between.

Fly on further

Send messages home

The sacrifice may never wake

Even in darkness

Even death

Is the hand up that you'll have to take.

There's a place there in fury

For all who believe

There's a chair at the foot of the bed

A reflection of angels connected in sleep

A scream as you reach for the end.

Travel with me

Take my lead

The winding of worlds goes unseen.

**Chapter 10: The death of a 9-year-old on the way to
school by debris from an exploding council house**

7 o'clock alarm bell rings
in mother's room
old legs fall to the lino cold,
think ahead and make all ready

7.05 the radio plays
the songs she listens to every day
she raises eyes to mother's smile
a uniform in the corner steady

7.30 clock does chime
breakfast eaten double quick
and feel the school bag weighs a brick
and all her friends are on their way

7.55 door shuts behind her
looks to see her mother's fine
she walks ahead as every time
and all the world before her

8 o'clock the house explodes
brick and tiles glass in the air

and after flight all falls to earth
and finds the girl and kills her there

and time now stops forever
the corner house in flames
the hands on the watch will never change
a waste, a second, then life goes on again

Chapter 11:   Blame Someone Else

Wake still alive,

my head cracked to the side,

sleep is stolen again

a Thursday in spring

don't they always just seem

as if winter has stayed

the alarm knows my name

I don't hear it

I sit in a field far away

tides lap around me,

their currents confuse me

as they play.

Such a frail thread

that we only knew

what you now must see

from that sea-weed throne

time held visions blurred

cataracts of sun

taming younger self

blaming someone else

cracked horizon trips

simple accidents

we can understand the end.

 Stuck to the door

breathing life through the holes

while it's moving away

after dawn comes the night

and the hard-melting drafts

but you ride them again

if there's really change coming

can't we just let the night

take its memories home

do you still break the glass

after toasting the king on your own?

such a strange road,

that I alone can lead

what you now must know,

on that dried up sea

simple sliding plains,

salt eyed waving lines

bring your refugee,

blaming someone else

soul in plastic frames,

simple cost of seed

we can understand the end.

Chapter 12: The Tree Knew

Behind my parents' home, put up in 1936

before the Blitz could knock it down,

there was a field,

my field.

I shared it - in truth - with a Mr. Watts

who rarely used it, if at all

and who was not aware he only held half.

The field was oblong, 2 acres square and worn.

It oozed as the Birket swelled each night,

a mirror field of puddles,

where thrush caught worms

and worms sought silence to be pecked.

To one side was the railway: *bachata* trains

each quarter hour,

and to the other identical homes and fences,

all roughly painted white,

that even Stukas could detect closed-eye.

I had three occupations.

The first was being out till dark.

The edges of the field where longer grass grew

were dens, collections, huts and tunnels at the sides.

This greying moss shot up within the dents

and later I would smoke the blades with nutmeg

and feel old.

Occasionally Mr. Watts erected posts both ends,

and I would train to kick the oval ball between.

Retrieving this allowed me to meet the neighbours

all at once,

for hours sitting till the shape came back.

The son called Scott poured frogs into a fire,

and watched them hiss and melt and nearly cried.

His dance of joy I still remember now,

the very tune to cruelty he was taught.

For months I kicked and kicked and missed and walked.

The mud and grass and business caked my shins.

I did not improve.

In a corner of my field stood a scaling tree, bent and open.

Its knots I filled with footprints and my lack of friend.

The tree knew.

Once my field was lent to others.

It filled with cars and trucks

and trough-destroying worlds.

The girl like string whose colour had been blanched

laid pins and nails and burst them as they came.

After that the rain alone slipped through the gate.

Apart from digging and kicking and odd fellows,

my second occupation was to be utterly alone.

The field flushed solitude from crowded homes.

Each blade of sod each bead of sweat was free.

I loved the fog there when it rose

from my old excavations.

Hidden we flew across to the second field,

the one that Watts held on his own.

The barrier a clump of weeds

all along from homes to rails,

and ankle deep and spat towards my socks.

The nettles and the clover wed in froth.

My tree had turned its wrinkles long before

and watched the other side of iron tracks.

One day I lay there in a tent with Scott.

It smelt of sick, I didn't sleep that night.

Once from much the same clump of oak

on that other side, came screams.

I wondered if my tree turned there in silent seeing

as their Mother.

The screams drew out into a thud and ceased.

My fog protects unless I would see out.

I heard a boy called Yann had disappeared,

but so much further down the line.

If they were his calls, they were mere echoes.

My other occupation was avoiding dogs,

for in this time they were everywhere.

The most evil given names which belie their true deceit,

like Sheba, Kaya or Therese,

to terrify the night with gums like rakes.

There was a point beyond which I could not creep

for fear of the old grey killer by the bricks,

enemy of milk-men and all courage.

The girl like string entangled in its beak.

A lady further up along the left owned

tiny screeching yellow things

she held like cherubim hold teats.

They snared her, barnacled in hate.

These odious things would not forsake her

for a meal of man.

Then Mr. Watts died.

My lonely mist a saviour more than once that day.

In 1936 the house still stood and shadowed

twice each morn the central ark

the sun had made one half to live in frost,

the other quarters jostled for his bones.

I was a bad child. I broke things. Not for pleasure
but,

for something in the mud.

In this and others I would at times team up as twins

with brother, whom our parents named just "boy".

The apples fallen in October were so hurled;

he west, I east and as we listened for the clash of
moans,

a greenhouse gives up underneath our rains

but none knew the source.

Here as we lay and laughed the Autumn from our
skin,

and prayed the judges blamed ill-luck,

the port and starboard put their hands on stones

and "boy" and I were daily crushed as beads.

The mud red with consequence. Yet none came.

So, Yann screamed; still the trains looped by,

and Yann screamed on and on and made dogs jump.

Beyond the houses was a small town then a sea.

After rails and trees were farms drawn back until a
top

on which stood The Beacon.

I loved the sea for its careless loss of time.

Any and every chagrin drew me sit before

and stare her out.

Such lives collect there reining in the chills

and always dark white, windy.

The grains of salt would clamour at my teeth.

I danced my eyes into her spume and cried

for what came next,

before we scuttled home

past milk-men,

loud and slow who never reach

but start again intact before they rise.

After his passing, the Watt's family

creeped out from a stone

and split his own heart all ways to suit theirs.

The school was sold off for flats.

The Headmaster's lodge became four more.

The first and second fields were kept as such by law,

but the third could turn a profit.

Men in yellow suits with tripods and with lines

scared the puddles into sight.

A vote was held in which Scott now old and bald and
foul

proposed that more new homes must surely be allowed

and he would build them.

His wife the girl like string now more a rope,

nodded on a hand-rubbed disk and smiled.

The figures leaping in her list of debts

that no one owed but all would sign.

Behind my parents' home, struck up in 1936

before the Blitz could count it down

stand four new houses glumly dashed

with fencing barbed along the tops.

The trains each hour or so, bash sense into their roots.

Its ice-berg goes on scratching the hull.

Scott and wife and dogs bark from the first,

and largest, closest to the scythe.

In one far garden walled as if the sky could cop a peak,

sits a girl alone, sullen face into her phone.

Her sister rocks upon my tree,

and coming from beneath,

I rot in silence.

She sings and listens to this thimbleful of dirt,

and wormless gravel keeping out the damp, but in.

And as a breeze comes echoed Yann

between his wagons, and the wires,

and now and then I tap her back,

to keep her swinging,

till the next raid sounds.

Chapter 13: All the seasons

A flock blew in from red skies far
The spring has come so soon again
Each bird a hope for sun and warmth
A change as winter nears its death

And all the waves still reach the shore
And all the rocks lie on the sand
And all the leaves blow on the ground
And all the seasons of each man

The flowers open in the snow
The bees did not appear till June
A hurricane replaced the breeze
That brought my heart to you

And all the boys laugh at my age
And all the men deny they'll die
And while our futures now are pasts
And bad times have become good-byes

Chapter 14: A Stranger

The man with hard bags knocked on every door
down our road

until one opened, which would never happen now,

and bade him in.

He placed his things hard on cold linoleum by the
Welsh dresser

in which bottles, spiked with beans were hidden from
the nurse,

and then he did what he had come to do,

and propped us up and robbed us of our light.

The man with dials whose banker must be blood,
pulled faces

until two, cup-foot, agitated and bewildered boys

stopped smiling and advanced into the frame.

What is memory if not time stuck

within the winding of a tooth?

The doused-out torch deletes its smoke into the suns

and stains my clouded child who cannot walk.

The man for one hour and a pound, ground furrows
in the rug.

The dripping lead and powder in the pipes; we drank
them in.

The boys, one named, both separate and caught.

One toy, one pose, two coppers for the tin.

Chapter 15: Carlton Lane

With the market road at one end and the railway at
the other,

Carlton Lane spanned the village and it let us
through.

A grim tube filled with moss, and the oil and stones
and holes

and dismal lack of lust left by the old season

and a failed dawn of shadows.

The laughably named Rose cottage was halfway on
the right

as I look.

Jennifer lives there and we are to marry.

Beyond this were garages for hire,

where Cortinas wept their lost suspension

diagonal and scrap,

among the vast spider kop clinging to their edge,

cannibals and no flies or roses of any description.

On from this space, and hacked in time, was the school house

erected by the Watts.

On the ground floor a gymnasium, then offices.

Above these classrooms and others that one never leaves.

Atop the lot were apartments filled with visitors and me.

In 1978 the power flicked. The parents roamed. A commotion.

In fear I kissed Sue Lawley on her screen,

then shook as drew-in vandals scanned the lane.

The noise they made still haunts me.

They are there.

Beneath the page.

Chapter 16: Ghosts

The ghosts that drift and waited in the chest,

who listened and obeyed and locked themselves in
dusk,

whose dust of steps made hangers fall inside,

and silent play around the bed conducting sleep.

The ghost which rocked about the breathless chair,

his chink of life, the darkness in the glass,

whose old spice clung and made her weep,

and hoped within the tunnels at the well.

The ghost that scared the child and closed the room,

her roses pruned and haunting on the frames,

whose wishes un-proclaimed become undone,

and strap her to this room and us.

The ghost of which we do not speak at all,

for living men must not become the pale.

One cannot hanker for the drop of boots,

while barring them at the door.

Chapter 17: The Shore

From Black point to the red rock, the limestone
breach to banks of sand,

the shore grew wrinkles for its worms to curl and dig.

Each coming wave replaced the next. The crabs
grieved salt,

would take away the edges of the moon.

The Irish girl who hid me in her loft at dawn, now
spent.

Her scales hung down and peeling in the east wind.

Before the first tide bends, the craft still turned away.

The wood prepares the measure of their age.

And my feet seize at the blinded shells and crush
their sleep to life.

There are still three miles ahead.

The gulls aligned and hungry for the catch, look up.
But no sky appears.

An old man with his first smoke at the lip,
a yellow cough in brine, his laugh. The dripping on a
boot.

He looms to the side and I greet him.
Another cloud.

When the hour comes and flashes in the black,
unwinding and the nest disturbed by flight.

The sudden cove whose creatures scuttle from the
light,

like old attractions.

Once the stone has been pulled shut,

There is no coda.

Chapter 18: First Love/Rock Ferry

Within my fog where miracles denied a break would
come,

obscuring growing man of seed beneath his cross,

came sudden dreams with girls inside the skip and
song

and tied me to a bulb.

The first girl tiny in her catholic name and syllables
and smiles,

curled raven hair around my neck and shook the nest
dry

and jealous of the space she moved.

The second in the church so plain I weaned her from
the blushing car,

but only saw my feet each mass we shuffled and
adored the sight.

The third shrub over-took the soil and grew a while

before the sun could kick it in.

All roots no petal, for the stamen withered in a
psalm.

The fourth destructive and unwound.

And after this the world around me glowed,

and shriveled in its praise.

I would be the last one picked out for the match.

Unskilled and so unblamed.

But by then it was too late

I was somehow man.

Then she came.

Chapter 19: The Middle Eye

These towns and villages are often adorned with epithets like "great" or "little".

Mine held the former but was not.

Only the gulls knew the truth that it was only

what the sea had no longer desired and had spat back.

Each new tide eroded the headland.

The shell beach had not yet been told of its greatness.

Neither had the buoys and posts which hovered and clanged like museums on the bank

and no one could remember what they said.

The slipways where sullen boys, worried mothers and irritated men

pushed craft into the sludge and waved.

It was deep enough to drown as many generations

had slithered to the quick sands;

a death one knew was frightful and yet preferable to old age in the Great village by the sea,

where others with your same name grew and grew,

and smoked and shrilled, as kippers on a slab,

looking out in suffocated, one-mouthed gasps
towards the islands.

Hildeburgh and her middle eye.

Only one with maps, and boots up to his throat,

and beards down to his chest, and without fear, knew
how.

The others are still out on the way, slightly below
your feet,

and their stumps move with the air,

and chatter and recoil from the worms,

the clicking posts and the gulls,

their witness.

www.ingramcontent.com/pod-product-compliance
Lightning Source LLC
Chambersburg PA
CBHW051400150726

48000CB00003B/1265